# Alone in the Arctic

by Diane Hoyt-Goldsmith
illustrated by Jill Kastner

## Scott Foresman

Editorial Offices: Glenview, Illinois • New York, New York
Sales Offices: Reading, Massachusetts • Duluth, Georgia
Glenview, Illinois • Carrollton, Texas • Menlo Park, California

With each step, George's foot broke through a crust of ice. Sinking up to his knees in the snow, George made slow progress. It was bitterly cold, but his efforts brought beads of sweat to his forehead.

One more mile to go, George thought. He gazed into the distance. He could just see the coastline. The steel blue of the ocean separated one white world from another. Sky and land were the same cold color.

This was George's first trip into the wilderness alone. He had taken a packet of medicine a few miles up the river to one of the elders. Her name was Elly. She was so stiff with arthritis that she had trouble getting to town. She lived with her husband, Roy, and a few old sled dogs.

That morning, his father had said, "You are twelve now. I guess you can handle a job like this. Please walk over to Elly's, but wear my parka so you'll be warm enough. Just give her this medicine and come right back. We have only a few hours of light today."

Getting there had been easy. The day was nice enough and there were only a few miles to go. George had said hello to Elly and Roy. He petted the dogs and gave Elly her medicine.

Then a wind blew up from the west. Clouds began to form over the ocean. The sky got dark.

"You'd better start back now, young fella." Roy said with a smile. "Here. Take these crackers and some muktuk. You might need a snack on the way home."

George took the packet of crackers and pieces of raw whale blubber. He put them in the pocket of his dad's parka. "Thanks," he said.

George and his family lived near Nome, Alaska, on the edge of the Arctic wilderness. They were Inupiat (IN-yoo-payt), which in their language means "the people." For centuries, people like George and his family have survived in the far north by understanding the obstacles they faced.

With the coming of winter, George knew that a storm could mean danger. He was in a hurry to get home.

Leaving Elly's place, George decided to take a shortcut across Moonrise Creek. When he got there, though, the creek was deeper than he had ever seen it and twice as wide. It was a bigger obstacle than he had imagined. Still, George was determined to cross it.

He spotted a few old tent poles left over
from a fishing camp. He picked one up. It was
long enough.

Then he gazed at the creek. A few large slabs
of ice were floating downstream. "That's just
what I need," he said to himself. He leaned over
and jabbed the wooden pole into the ice. He
pulled it over to the bank. Then he stepped onto
it.

The piece of ice made a perfect raft. Slowly,
using all his strength, George poled his way
across the swollen creek. But it was tough going.
George fought the rushing current for each inch.

From the other bank of the creek, George had to climb up a steep hill. The wind came up suddenly. It blew snow into his eyes. Halfway up, George stepped on a slick rock. He slipped and fell, rolling all the way to the bottom of the hill.

Groaning, George checked himself carefully for injuries. His leg hurt so much he thought it might be sprained or broken. His cheek was sore. It bled a little where he had scraped it on the ice. And the storm was getting worse.

He'd lived all his life on the edge of the wilderness. George knew he had to do something fast. He wasn't far from home. But the storm was fierce. When weather overtakes an Arctic traveler, it can be dangerous. With his injuries, he knew it would be hard for him to walk. For a moment, his mind ran wild. He could only think the worst kinds of thoughts.

Then, suddenly, as if in a dream, George saw the face of his grandfather. He heard his grandfather's voice, soft and slow. He was telling stories about his childhood. He told about being lost in a storm. Grandfather told how he built up a pile of rocks. He stacked them one on top of another until they made a small tower. His family found the tower, and Grandfather too.

The memory gave George an idea. But first he had to do something about his leg. He took his jackknife out of his pocket. He cut into the white canvas parka cover. He tore off a strip of cloth. He wrapped it around his leg. It took a long time because George was in so much pain.

Meanwhile, it got colder and darker. The wind began to howl. Snow began to whirl. Soon the storm was roaring all around him. Ice crystals stuck to his face like shiny needles. George set to work. Hobbling on his hurt leg, he collected flat stones that were small enough to lift and carry. He brought ten or twelve to the top of an icy snow bank. He stacked them there until they took the shape of a person. There was even a little round stone for a head.

Then George took out his jackknife. He used it to carve out some ice from the crust that covered the snow bank. Then he dug into the snow like a dog. He scooped out a hole just big enough for his body. His grandfather said snow can keep you warm in a bad storm. It traps air as it falls. The air helps insulate you from the cold.

When the hole was large enough, George crawled inside and sat down. Once he was out of the wind, George was surprised that he didn't feel cold. His leg ached. "I can stand it," he said to himself. He had to.

Soon it was totally dark. The wind was howling and snow was piling up all around.

George felt his heart beating in his chest. His thoughts were filled with confusion. This happens sometimes when fear overtakes a person. George began to feel frightened and alone.

He put his hand into his pocket to get a cracker. He felt something smooth.

He took it out of his pocket. It was a small seal carved from a walrus tusk. His father always carried it with him when he went hunting. He told George that it brought good luck.

The little seal was very old. George knew that his grandfather had carved it one winter long ago. He had heard the story of how Grandfather had given the seal to his father when he was a boy.

They had gone seal hunting that day. George's father harpooned his first seal. George's father had learned his lessons well. He had crawled over the ice, trying to look and act like a seal. When he was in range, he had thrown the harpoon and hit the seal. Later, he gave the seal meat to one of the elders in the village. On that day, George's grandfather was very proud.

George was suddenly very tired. He closed his eyes. His fist closed over the little seal and he fell asleep.

The next thing he knew, his father and mother were shaking him.

"Wake up, George," they cried. "Are we ever glad to find you! We saw the rock pile you made, even in this awful storm. We knew you had to be close by."

The next time George woke up he was in his own bed. His body ached all over and he was thirsty.

"Have some water, son," his father said. He handed George a glass.

George noticed that the little seal was on the table next to his bed.

"Where did you find this?" he asked.

"You had it in your hand when we found you," his father answered. "I want you to have it. You proved to me that you are quite grown up now. Not everyone has the courage to take care of things the way you did. You made very sensible decisions out there!"

George looked over at the little seal and smiled.